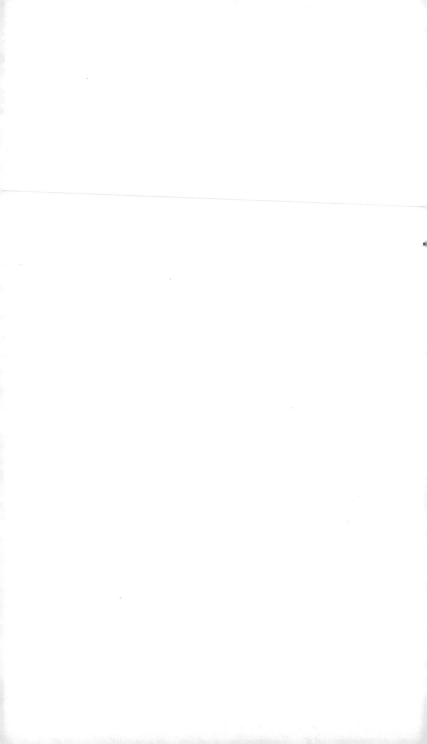

The
Latchkey Dog

Also by Mary Jane Auch:
Angel and Me and the Bayside Bombers

The Latchkey Dog

by Mary Jane Auch

Illustrated by Cat Bowman Smith

Little, Brown and Company

Boston   New York   Toronto   London

Text copyright © 1994 by Mary Jane Auch
Illustrations copyright © 1994 by Cat Bowman Smith

First Edition

The characters and events portrayed in this book are fictitious. Any similarity to real persons, living or dead, is coincidental and not intended by the author.

Library of Congress Cataloging-in-Publication Data

Auch, Mary Jane.
  The latchkey dog / by Mary Jane Auch ; illustrated by Cat Bowman Smith.—1st ed.
    p. cm.
  Summary: Sam's efforts to help his dog, Amber, adjust to being home alone all day cause his mother to worry that Sam is spending too much time by himself.
  ISBN 0-316-05916-1
  [1. Dogs—Fiction. 2. Latchkey children—Fiction. 3. Single-parent family—Fiction.] I. Smith, Cat Bowman, ill. II. Title.
PZ7.A898Lat 1994
[Fic]—dc20   93-18604

10 9 8 7 6 5 4 3 2 1

RRD-VA

Published simultaneously in Canada
by Little, Brown & Company (Canada) Limited

Printed in the United States of America

For Gail Heimberger — the kind of teacher every kid should have!

The
Latchkey Dog

Chapter One

I could hear the racket the minute my sister Maxie and I got off the school bus. It wasn't just my dog, Amber, barking. Two soap operas and a rock band were blasting from the windows of our house.

Our next-door neighbor was waiting for us. "You're deliberately trying to drive me crazy, aren't you, Sam?"

"No, honest, Mrs. Watson." I fumbled with my house key, jamming it into the lock. "I don't know why Amber's still barking."

"If she has any sense, she's trying to drown out the noise in your house."

"I didn't think the TVs were on that loud." Now I could hear thumps on the door as Amber threw herself against it from the inside.

"Stay back when I open the door, Maxie. Amber's so excited to see us, she'll knock you right over."

Mrs. Watson leaned out over her porch railing. "You're not going to tell me that dog of yours watches TV, Sam."

"Not exactly. I left the radios and TVs on so Amber would think someone was home with her. She only barks because she's lonesome."

We'd been having problems with Amber ever since Mom started her job. Amber just hated to be left alone.

Mrs. Watson glared at me. "I'm at my wit's end. If you can't keep that dog quiet, she'll have to go. There are laws about disturbing the peace, you know."

There are laws against being mean to kids and animals, too, I thought, pushing the door open.

I'd barely gotten inside when Amber pounced on me, sending my books skidding across the floor. She knocked me down, then slathered my face with kisses. How could I get

4

rid of a dog who loved me as much as Amber did?

Mrs. Watson was always complaining about something. My best friend, Jamie Diggs, said that's what people were like when they got old. I believed Jamie, because his father's a psychologist, and Dr. Diggs knows just about everything.

Mom got home a few minutes later. Mrs. Watson barreled over as soon as Mom's car pulled into the driveway. I tried to listen from my room, but I couldn't catch what they were saying. When I heard Mrs. Watson leave, I ran downstairs.

"We have a problem, Sam," Mom said. "Your plan to keep Amber from being lonesome didn't work. I'm afraid we'll have to give her up."

"Mom! When we got Amber, you were the one who said you adopt a dog for keeps."

"Back then, your father was still with us and I was at home all day."

"It's not Amber's fault that you and Dad got

5

divorced. Why can't you quit your job and stay home again?"

Mom put her hands on my shoulders. "Sam, you know I have to work to help support us now. We've been over this a dozen times."

I knew it couldn't really happen, Mom staying home again. I just wanted our life to be the way it was before. Too many things were changing. "Can't we wait, Mom? Amber will get used to being alone if we just give her a little time."

"Mrs. Watson wants something done right away." Mom leaned down and scratched Amber behind the ears. "This isn't easy for me either, Sam. Amber and I have spent a lot of time together. But she isn't happy, and we need to find a new home for her. I'm going to call the paper to put in an ad."

"How do we know the people who take her will be good to her? How do we know they're not just going to tie her up in an old shed or something?"

Mom sat down at the kitchen table and

startęd writing. "We'll say right in the ad that Amber loves people and needs lots of attention."

"She loves *us*," I said. "You can't just say that she loves people, because we may be the only people in the whole world that she even likes. Did you ever think of that?"

Mom kept writing. "I think Amber will be perfectly happy with anyone who feeds her and scratches her behind the ears. Besides, even you don't spend as much time with Amber as you used to, Sam. If you're not at school, you're over at Jamie's house."

Amber nuzzled my hand and whined, as if she knew we were talking about her. "Mrs. Watson should just mind her own business," I said. "She's the one causing all the problems."

"Mrs. Watson has more on her mind than you realize," Mom said. "Mr. Watson seems to be getting more absentminded every day. I know she worries when he wanders off."

"I'd wander off, too, if I lived with Mrs. Watson," I said.

"Well, don't wander off now. I need you to keep an eye on your sister while I run out for a few groceries, okay?"

"Aw, Mom. I don't want to be stuck in the house. Amber needs to get some exercise."

"You don't have to stay in the house. Maxie's engrossed in her favorite TV show. Just make sure you stay in the yard in case she needs you."

"Sure, Mom." I took Amber out in the backyard and threw the Frisbee around for her. She still hadn't learned how to catch a Frisbee on the fly. Each time, she let it hit the ground before she grabbed it. Then I had to chase her all over the yard before she'd let me have it again.

Pretty soon Mr. Watson peeked over the fence. "Hi, Sam. How's it going?"

"Not so great." I pried the slimy Frisbee from Amber's mouth. "Did Mrs. Watson tell you she's making us give Amber away?"

Mr. Watson's face got serious as he came through the gate. He bent down and took Amber's face in his hands. "How could anyone

9

give away such a beautiful dog?" Amber wagged her tail so hard her whole body wiggled.

Suddenly I had a great idea. Giving Amber away to somebody I knew wouldn't be half as bad as sending her off with a stranger. "Do you want Amber, Mr. Watson? She really likes you. I can tell."

"I've missed having a dog." Mr. Watson gazed off into the distance. "Did I ever tell you about the dog I had when I was your age?"

He'd told me about a hundred times, but I didn't want to hurt his feelings, so I shook my head.

"My dog, Midnight, was a lot like Amber," Mr. Watson said. "Of course he was black instead of gold, and had short legs instead of long, and his ears stood up instead of hanging down . . . but he looked a lot like Amber."

"Just think, Mr. Watson — if you take Amber, it'll be like having your old dog back. You can even call her Midnight if you want to. Amber's real smart. She'll catch on that you're talking to her."

I could see by the look in Mr. Watson's eyes that I was winning him over. When Mrs. Watson saw how much her husband wanted a dog, she couldn't possibly say no. This was just like the old days, when I'd talk Dad into something I wanted to do before I asked Mom. Then it was two against one, and we almost always convinced her.

From the look on Mr. Watson's face, I could tell he was picturing himself as Amber's new owner, so I kept quiet. "It would be like having Midnight back again," Mr. Watson said finally. "Okay, Sam. I'll take her."

"And you'll let me visit her every day, right?" I asked.

"Sure, anytime. Come on, boy." He slapped the side of his leg and headed for the gate. I thought he was talking to me until he turned and said, "You, too, Sam. Let's show Midnight his new home."

Chapter Two

Amber trotted along beside Mr. Watson, her tail doing wild figure eights. As soon as we got into the house, Mr. Watson headed for the refrigerator. He pulled the wrapping off a frozen steak and tossed it to Amber. She caught it before it hit the floor. Why couldn't she do that with a Frisbee?

"Are you sure she . . . he . . . should have that?" I asked. "Shouldn't it be thawed out first?"

Mr. Watson shook his head. "Won't hurt him. Just think of it as a doggie Popsicle." He went over to the hall closet and pulled out a green coat. "This should do just fine for Midnight."

Was he kidding? I knew some people put

fancy jackets on their dogs, but Amber wasn't used to that. My sister, Maxie, had tried to dress her up in one of her baby dresses once. Amber had taken off and come back an hour later with the dress hanging in shreds around her. Maxie cried and carried on the rest of the night, but it was her own fault for doing something so stupid.

I was just about to warn Mr. Watson about putting the coat on Amber when he took a laundry basket off a kitchen chair and dumped the clothes on the floor. Then he arranged the coat in the bottom of the basket. "Here you go, boy. Jump in."

For a second there I almost made a fool of myself. Amber knew who he meant, though. She trotted over and plunked herself in the basket, still chomping on the steak.

"He remembers," Mr. Watson said, smiling. "He used to have a bed just like this."

"Mr. Watson?" I tugged gently at his sleeve. "This is really my dog, Amber, and she's a girl. I mean she's your dog now, and you can call

her Midnight but . . ." I didn't know what else to say, and when I looked at Mr. Watson's face, I was sorry I'd said that much. He looked so sad for a minute, I thought he might cry.

Then he pulled back his shoulders and smiled. "A dog always seems like a *he* to me. A cat, now that's a *she*. Hard to figure out, just like a woman. But a dog can be your best friend, right, Midnight?"

Amber didn't seem to care what Mr. Watson called her. She had the steak propped up between her paws, and her head was tilted way over to one side so she could chew on it with her sharp back teeth. The thawed part of the meat was dripping blood on the coat. Mr. Watson pulled up a chair and sat watching her. I'd never seen him look so happy. My plan had worked. I decided to get out of there so Amber could get used to her new home.

"Well, I guess I'd better be going," I said. Neither of them looked up, so I started to let myself out the side door.

That's when I ran into Mrs. Watson. She almost dropped her grocery bag, but I caught it. "Thanks, Sam. I didn't expect to find you here." Her eyes went past me to the laundry basket. "What's that dog doing in here? Walter, that's the steak I bought for our Sunday dinner!"

"Don't worry, dear. I'm only letting him eat my half. You'll still have the rest for your dinner. A hot dog will do just fine for me."

Mrs. Watson lunged for the steak, but Amber growled and snapped at her hand. "Good heavens! That vicious dog tried to bite me!"

"I don't think Midnight's finished my half of the steak yet," Mr. Watson said.

Amber was half standing in the basket, gulping frozen hunks of steak while she glared at Mrs. Watson.

"Walter! Is that my good wool coat she's lying on?"

"I didn't think you'd mind, dear. You haven't worn it in months."

"Of course I haven't been wearing it!" Mrs.

Watson shouted. "It's been seventy degrees outside, and this is a winter coat. And look at my clean laundry all over the floor! Are you out of your mind?"

Amber started barking at her, dropping the last of the steak. I grabbed it and picked up the leash. "Here, Mrs. Watson. If you cut the teeth marks off, this should still be okay."

I'm not sure what she yelled at us, because we didn't stay around to listen, but the steak sailed by us as we ran down the driveway. Amber tried to scarf it up, but I yanked at her leash and kept going. I wanted to get as far away from Mrs. Watson as possible. We didn't stop until we got to the beach at the end of our road.

I sat on a log that had washed up during the last big storm on the lake. "What was the matter with you back there, Amber? You never acted like that before."

Amber whined softly. She could tell I was mad at her.

"I don't blame you for wanting to bite Mrs.

18

Watson. I'd like to bite her myself. But you got us into a real mess now. Mrs. Watson is going to be putting more pressure than ever on Mom to get rid of you."

Amber wasn't paying any attention to me. She was too busy watching a bunch of sea gulls fight over a bag of potato chips down the beach.

"I don't know why I worry about you anyway. You sure made yourself right at home at the Watsons. Are you going to miss me as much as I'll miss you?"

Amber strained at the leash, trembling with the urge to chase sea gulls. I unhitched her, and she dashed off, barking and leaping at the sky as the gulls circled and scolded above her.

Probably if Amber had a hunk of steak and a bunch of sea gulls, she wouldn't care where she lived. I cared, though. I had to find someone else to take her — someone I knew. I couldn't let her go to strangers.

"Jamie!" I shouted. "He thinks you're terrific, Amber. Besides, his father is home all day because his office is right in the house. It's perfect."

As soon as I could catch Amber and hook her leash up, we ran over to Jamie's house. Jamie thought taking Amber was a great idea, but Dr. Diggs didn't. "I'm sorry, Sam, but I just don't like dogs. I'm told I was bitten by a dog when I was very young. It's left me with a canine phobia."

"Amber doesn't bite, Dr. Diggs. She loves people."

"Why is she baring her teeth like that?" Dr. Diggs asked, putting a chair between himself and the dog.

"She's smiling. She likes you."

"I have a patient due any minute. You have to get Amber out of here. Perhaps if you reprogram your dog, you can solve her problem."

"I don't think anybody ever programmed her in the first place," I said.

"I know what Dad's talking about," Jamie said. "Positive reinforcement, right, Dad?"

Dr. Diggs was standing on the chair now. Amber was nibbling at his shoelaces. "That's right, son. It's the best method for teaching both animals and humans. Now . . . um . . . take Sam and his dog back home and tell them all about it."

"Your dad sure has a hang-up about dogs," I said when we got outside.

"He's scared of all kinds of animals," Jamie

21

said. "That's why I have a Venus flytrap for a pet. Dad was never bitten by a plant."

"So what's this positive . . . you know."

Jamie pushed his glasses back up. "Positive reinforcement. It just means you reward the behavior you're trying to encourage."

"You sound like your father," I said. "Tell me in plain English."

"Every time Amber does what you want her to, you give her something she likes."

"You mean like a dog biscuit?"

Jamie nodded. "That should work."

When we got back to the house, Maxie was sitting on the front steps. "You're in big trouble, Sam. Wait till I tell Mom you ran off and left me all alone."

I wasn't used to being responsible for Maxie. I wasn't used to a lot of things that were happening now that we didn't have Mom home all the time. But I couldn't admit to Maxie that I'd forgotten all about her. "I didn't run off," I said. "I was just down at Jamie's for a minute."

"That's running off," Maxie said. "Mom told

you not to leave me alone, even for a minute. I'm telling."

I reached in my pocket and found the candy bar I'd saved from lunch. "If you promise not to tell, I'll let you have this."

Maxie's eyes lit up. "Okay, but next time I'm telling." She grabbed the candy bar and ran into the backyard.

"Now she'll bug you all the time," Jamie said.

"Why?"

"Because you just rewarded her for bugging you. It's just like Amber. Positive reinforcement."

"Forget about her," I said, pulling a new box of dog biscuits out of the cupboard. "What am I supposed to do with Amber?"

Jamie sat down at the kitchen table and folded his arms. He looked just like his father. "Every time Amber does what you want her to, you give her a dog biscuit."

"I want her to keep quiet."

Jamie nodded. "And she's quiet right now, so reward her."

I gave Amber the biscuit, and she chomped it down. Then she looked at me, tail wagging. "Now what do I do?"

"She's still being quiet," Jamie said. "Give her another biscuit."

I did. Amber was smiling now. "How many should I give her?"

"Just give her one every few minutes."

"When do I stop?"

"When she barks."

Amber never barked all afternoon.

Mom was mad at me when she got home. First she was mad because I used up two whole boxes of dog biscuits.

Then she was even madder — when Amber threw up all over the living room rug.

Chapter Three

Things went back to normal over the weekend. Amber was happy because we were all home, and there was no barking for Mrs. Watson to complain about. I figured the problem with Amber would go away if I didn't remind anybody about it.

On Monday, the phone was ringing as I unlocked the door. It was Mom. "Sam, I'm still at work. I have to finish up something here before I can leave. Will you and Maxie be all right?"

"Sure, Mom, but I wanted to go over to Jamie's."

"I'm working as fast as I can, Sam. Just stay there with Maxie until I get home. I won't be much longer."

25

I called Jamie. Maxie was wobbling around in Mom's high heels and had one of her dolls clutched in her arms. "I'm the mommy, and you be the daddy, Sam. This is our little girl, Lurlene. She wants Daddy to take her for a walk in the backyard."

"Quit bugging me, will you? Jamie and I have important business to discuss."

"Lurlene's crying," she said, shoving the doll in my face. "See? *Waaah!* Daddy doesn't want to play with me. *Waaaah!*"

"Knock it off! Not you, Jamie. Maxie's being a pain. Yeah, you were right about giving her the candy bar."

"You're supposed to play with me until Mom gets home," Maxie whined.

"There was nothing in the deal about me playing house. I'm just here to call 911 if you fall out of the attic window or something. And I'm only calling if I see blood, so don't try to fake it just to get attention."

Maxie sat down in the middle of the living room and started wailing. Amber was running

in circles around her, barking. Amber couldn't stand to see anybody cry. She didn't notice that Maxie was crying without tears. I couldn't hear Jamie over all the noise. "I'll be over later!" I shouted into the receiver.

Maxie stopped crying the instant I hung up the phone. "Look, Lurlene. Daddy's going to play with you now." She shoved the doll into my hands.

I held the doll up in front of me. "Lurlene, tell your mommy if she doesn't stop bugging me, I'm going to get a divorce and move far away."

Maxie grabbed her doll back from me. She didn't cry out loud this time, but her eyes filled with tears. "That was really mean, Sam." She turned and went up to her room, hugging the doll tight to her chest.

I didn't have time to feel bad about what I'd said, because I heard Mom's car.

"Sorry about being late," she said, dumping a pile of folders on the table. "I'm afraid I'm going to be even later tomorrow. My boss is having me reorganize the whole computer system. The person who had my job last must have been from the Middle Ages. She barely used the computers. I'll call around to find a baby-sitter."

"I don't need a baby-sitter in the middle of the day, Mom. It would be embarrassing."

"That may be, but I'll still need a sitter for Maxie. By the way, were there any calls about the ad?"

"What ad?" I asked.

"Sam, I told you we had to find a new home for Amber."

"But not so soon!" I yelled. "You didn't even give me a chance to look."

"You're not going to find a home by walking around the neighborhood. The newspaper ad will reach hundreds of people."

"Sure, strangers! I want Amber to live with somebody I know, so I can visit her."

Mom put her arm around me. "That would be perfect, Sam, but it probably won't happen. All we can do is make sure whoever takes Amber will be kind to her."

"I'm not giving up yet, Mom. I'm going over to Jamie's. I have an idea, and he might be able to help me."

Dr. Diggs answered the door. He wouldn't let me in until he was sure I didn't have Amber with me.

Jamie was up in his room, feeding a fly to his plant, Vera. "Any luck getting rid of Amber yet?" he asked.

"I don't want to get rid of her. I'm trying to keep her."

Jamie shrugged. "I think it's a losing battle.

29

What you need is a low-maintenance pet like Vera. No barking, no mess. I just have to catch flies for her every few days."

I watched Vera clamp down on the fly with her spiny leaf. "Yeah, Vera's just loaded with personality. Listen, I have an idea about Amber. She's bored, right?"

Jamie put Vera back on the windowsill. "I suppose so."

"What if we found a job for her? Lots of dogs work as Seeing Eye dogs or drug sniffers for the police."

"That's stupid, Sam. Those dogs go through months of training."

"So maybe she wouldn't have an actual job. Maybe she could just be a volunteer."

"Sam, think! Even if we could find a job for Amber, how would she get to it? Take the bus?"

"My mom could drop her off on the way to work and pick her up on the way home," I said. "I know she wouldn't mind. She's only giving Amber away because she can't think of what else to do."

Jamie rubbed his chin the same way his father does when he's thinking. "Only a small percentage of dogs ever have jobs. I bet it's not more than one in a hundred. Maybe even a thousand."

"But Amber's one in a million," I said. "She's really smart. All we need to do is find the right job for her. She'll do the rest."

Jamie sat down at his computer. "Okay, I have a program that tells what kind of work you're suited for. It's not meant for dogs, but it might give us some leads." He pushed a few buttons, and a list of questions appeared on the screen. "What are Amber's favorite things to do?"

"Eat and chase squirrels."

Jamie typed something, and the computer beeped. "They don't have 'Chasing squirrels,' but they have 'Enjoys handling food.' What else?"

31

"Chewing bones, barking at sea gulls, riding in the car . . ."

The computer beeped again. "No bones or sea gulls, but I can put the car under 'Enjoys travel.' Anything else?"

"Okay, she likes running on the beach, playing Frisbee, catching balls . . ."

Another beep. Jamie typed something else. "That sounds like she's 'Athletically inclined.'"

"I guess so, for a dog."

"Okay, 'Enjoys contact with people.' On a scale of one to five, she's a five, right?"

"She's a ten."

Jamie pushed a few more buttons, and the computer made a series of beeps. "Your troubles are over. You have not one, but two choices."

"What are they?"

Jamie leaned back in his chair and smiled. "She could be a trainer in a fitness center or an airline flight attendant."

Chapter Four

When I got home from Jamie's, there was a strange car in our driveway.

A lady was sitting in the living room with Mom. "Sam," Mom said, "you're going to be so pleased. This is Mrs. Rumsey. She saw the ad, and she's thinking about taking Amber."

"We just live in the next block," Mrs. Rumsey said. "And I work at home, so Amber wouldn't get lonesome. You could come visit her as often as you like."

"That would be nice," I said, but I didn't mean it. I didn't want Amber going to anybody else, no matter how close they lived. Acting friendly might buy me a little time, though. It would give me a chance to think of a plan.

"Mrs. Rumsey's daughter is getting acquainted with Amber out back, Sam. Why don't you go out to meet her?"

That was it! I'd convince this girl that Amber bites people. Nobody wants a dog who bites.

I was halfway down the back steps when the name Rumsey rang a bell. Rumsey! A girl named Meredith Rumsey had had a crush on me since kindergarten, and she was a major pain in the neck.

"Hi, Samuel!" Sure enough, it was her. Meredith Rumsey was the only person in the world who called me Samuel. "Isn't this just wonderful?" she gushed. "We're going to take your dog, and you can come over to my house every day to see her, Samuel."

"I wouldn't get my hand that close to Amber's mouth if I were you," I said.

"Why not?"

"Didn't my mother tell you? She bites."

Meredith laughed. "Your mother bites?"

"Very funny. I'm talking about the dog. You won't be laughing when she lops a couple of your fingers off."

"Don't be silly," Meredith said. "I've been playing with her for over half an hour. She's the sweetest dog I ever saw."

"Not when she's in a bad mood," I said.

Meredith ignored my remark. "On the days you can't come over, I'll bring Amber to visit you." She batted her eyelashes at me. "Isn't this fun, Samuel? We'll be like Amber's mother and father."

Things were getting out of control. Not only was I losing Amber, but Meredith would be bugging me all the time. I had to get out of there. "Gotta go do my homework," I said.

Meredith called after me, "But we don't have any homework, Samuel," as I bolted through the door and up the stairs.

I hid out in my closet until I heard the Rumseys' car start up. Then I ran downstairs. "Mom!" I yelled. "We have to talk."

Mom was holding the front door open with her shoulder, waving to the Rumseys. "They're nice people, don't you think, Sam? I'm sure Meredith will take good care of Amber, and you'll be able to see her whenever you want to."

"But I can't stand Meredith, Mom. She's the last person I want to give my dog to. Can't we wait until we find someone better?"

"I'm sorry you feel that way, Sam, but we can't very well go back on our offer now."

"What do you mean, *our* offer? You're the one who put the ad in the paper. Besides, if Amber's my dog, I should be the one to choose where she goes."

"I think we're lucky to have even one answer to our ad, Sam. It just happened that

Meredith's father had promised her a dog for her birthday. He's already fencing in their backyard. They want to take her next weekend."

"He promised her *a* dog, not *my* dog. They can find one at the animal shelter. They have tons of dogs that nobody wants."

"By the way, Sam, I've called everyone I can think of. I couldn't get a baby-sitter for tomorrow. You'll have to watch Maxie until I get home."

"Okay," I said, "but if I do that for you, will you tell Meredith she can't have my dog?"

Mom plugged in the vacuum cleaner and turned it on. "I'm not giving up on the Rumseys unless someone else comes to answer the ad," she shouted over the vacuum's roar. "We're at the end of our rope here." She always started vacuuming when she was tired of arguing with me.

I ran upstairs, called Jamie, and told him what was happening.

Jamie snorted. "That's great. I'm sure you

and Meredith will make wonderful parents, *Samuel*."

"Jamie, this is an emergency. What if Mom's right about nobody else answering the ad? Besides, I don't want to give Amber up. She's been around as long as I can remember. There must be some way to keep her quiet during the day so we don't have to give her away. I have less than two weeks to come up with a plan. Help me think of something."

"I've used up all my ideas," Jamie said.

"Just try to think. Even if it sounds like the dumbest idea in the whole world."

There was a long silence. "Well . . . I read once that dogs who are raised with cats tend to be quieter, and sleep more during the day."

"What good does that do us, Jamie? Amber wasn't raised with a cat."

"Maybe we can give her a crash course. I'm feeding the Andersons' cat while they're on vacation. I could bring her over to your house. When Amber sees how the cat sleeps all the time, maybe she'll take the hint."

"Jamie, are you nuts? Cats and dogs spend their whole lives plotting how to make each other miserable."

Jamie cleared his throat. "I read about this in one of my father's psychology books. You think you know more than the doctor who wrote it?"

"You win," I said. "We can do it right after school. My mom said she's going to be late getting home."

I hurried home from school the next day. I had to get Maxie out of the way so she couldn't tell Mom about our borrowing the Andersons' cat. "Guess what, Maxie? You're going to play over at Lisa Swartman's house today."

Maxie looked suspicious. "Did Mommy say it was okay?"

"Well, it was my idea," I said. "You can take Lurlene with you and play Mommies at the Playground on Lisa's swing set."

"Did Lisa's mommy say it was okay?"

I hadn't thought about calling Mrs. Swartman, but I didn't have time to mess around. Jamie would be here any minute with the cat.

"Come on," I said, grabbing her hand. We practically ran all the way down the block to the Swartmans' house. Nobody answered the bell, so I pounded on the door.

"They're not home," Maxie said. "The car's gone."

I grabbed Maxie's hand, and we ran back home.

"You lied, Sam. You said I could play at Lisa's."

"I'll read to you instead," I said. I took her up to her room and grabbed a boring-looking book from Mom's bookcase. Maxie snuggled into her pillow. I started to read in a low, dull voice and had to stop every now and then to sound out the long words. "A vector and its two com . . . com-po . . . nents . . . components form a right triangle."

I could see Maxie's eyes fluttering. Then

they finally closed. I tiptoed out of her room, closing the door slowly so the click of the latch wouldn't wake her up.

Amber was asleep on the hall rug. When I wanted to be boring, I could knock out everybody in the house.

"You're going to have a visitor today, Amber," I whispered. "A nice quiet visitor."

Amber woke up and followed me downstairs, her tail thumping against the wall. About ten minutes later, the doorbell rang, and Amber started barking. I held on to her collar and opened the door. Jamie was holding the biggest cat I'd ever seen in my life.

"This is Iris," he said. Iris took one look at Amber and scrambled onto Jamie's head. Her tail puffed up like a bottle brush.

"Yeeeow!" Jamie yelled. "Get this cat off me! Her claws are digging into my scalp!"

"Let me put Amber away first," I said. I dragged her by the collar. It took all of my strength to shove her into the downstairs bathroom and get the door closed behind her.

When I got back into the living room, Jamie was still wearing Iris like a big Davy Crockett coonskin cap. Her tail draped over Jamie's left eye.

I carefully peeled Iris off Jamie's head. "I don't think this is going to work."

Jamie straightened out his glasses. "Yes, it will. We just have to get Iris calmed down." He got on the floor with the cat. "Go to sleep, Iris. Nice kitty."

Iris looked around the room. Her ears were so flat against her head, she looked like she was wearing a bathing cap.

"Iris doesn't seem to be dozing off," I said.

"Lie in front of the cat and pretend you're sleeping," Jamie said. "Breathe real slow."

I was pretty sure this wouldn't work, but I didn't have any better ideas. A low growl was coming from deep in Iris's throat.

All of a sudden Maxie came running down the stairs.

"Oh, no — I forgot she was home," I said. Jamie grabbed one of Iris's hind legs as she tried to dive under the couch.

Maxie heard Amber barking, so she opened the door to the downstairs bathroom. A huge white figure bolted into the room. "It's the

43

Mummy from the Lost Crypt!" Maxie screamed. "Just like on TV."

"It's just Amber," I said. "She must have gotten tangled up in the toilet paper." I threw my whole body over Amber to hold her down. She was inching her way toward Iris, dragging me and two throw rugs across the floor with her.

"Look at the kitty! Can I have her?" Maxie lunged for Iris. Jamie lost his grip on the cat. Iris streaked across the room and clawed her way up the drapes.

"Now look what you've done!" I yelled. I caught the curtain rod as it fell, but not before it knocked over a lamp. "Go back to your room, Maxie. And stay there. I can't solve the problem with Amber and baby-sit you, too."

"You're not the boss of me!" Maxie shouted. "When Mom gets home, I'm telling her everything."

I didn't have to worry about Maxie telling on me. In the middle of the whole mess, the door opened, and there was Mom.

She was madder than I had ever seen her. She even yelled at Jamie before she sent Iris and him home. Then she turned to me. "Sam, you are hereby grounded for the rest of your life."

"But Mom! You have to let me explain."

Mom plunked me onto the couch. Then she sat in the chair across from me and folded her arms. "All right, Sam. Start talking. And this had better be good."

The plan that had seemed almost sensible when Jamie came up with it sounded ridiculous now. Mom didn't interrupt me, but I could tell she wasn't impressed.

Neither was Maxie. "You can't make a dog think she's a cat, Sam. That's the dumbest thing I ever heard."

"Oh, yeah? Well, I don't see you doing anything to solve our problem, so you're the stupid one. Besides, I'm sick of having to baby-sit you."

"You aren't my baby-sitter!" Maxie shouted. "I'm not a baby. I'm big, aren't I, Mommy?"

Maxie ran over and climbed into Mom's lap.

Mom looked really tired all of a sudden. "Listen, both of you. This family has to start working together. Sam, don't you understand that I need you to be responsible for yourself and Maxie on the days that I'm late getting home? Is that asking too much?"

"No," I mumbled.

"Good," Mom said. "Just to make sure you don't forget, you're grounded for a week. And I'm going to make other arrangements for you after school. This just isn't working out."

I didn't argue with her. It was better than being grounded for the rest of my life. It wasn't fair, though. I was just a kid. Why did I have to be responsible for my dog *and* my little sister?

Jamie was lucky. He didn't have to worry about anything but a plant.

Chapter Five

In the middle of math the next day, I had this terrific idea. I started to tell Jamie at lunch.

"I don't want to hear any more great ideas about Amber," Jamie said, unwrapping his sardine sandwich. "Your last one almost killed me."

"The last idea was yours," I said. "And it almost killed me, too, so you owe me one. Call your dad and see if you can sleep over tonight."

"Why?"

"We're going to keep Amber awake all night. Then she'll conk out and sleep all day tomorrow."

"So will we," Jamie said. "Besides, even if it worked, we couldn't do it every night."

"We won't have to. People have this little internal clock. When they go to a new time zone it takes a day for the clock to reset itself to the new time. It happened to us when we went to visit my grandmother in Colorado. We kept waking up two hours early every morning."

"So?"

"So if we keep Amber up all night, it would be like taking her to a different time zone. Her internal clock will think night is day and day is night. After tonight, Amber will sleep like a baby while she's alone."

"Interesting scientific experiment," Jamie said. "Okay, let's try it."

We got permission from the lunch monitor to go to the main office so Jamie could call home. While Jamie was dialing, Mrs. Insalaca, the school secretary, gave me the evil eye. "What are you plotting now, Sam? You don't have any more surprises up your sleeve, do you?"

"Me?" I said, trying to look innocent.

Why is it that adults only remember the times you mess up? Last year I'd had this really great idea about recycling bottle caps. I figured if they could recycle the bottles, they could recycle the caps. After all, who wants the whole earth cluttered up with bottle caps, right? So I told all my friends about it and they told all their friends. We all saved up as many bottle caps as we could all year and brought them in to school on April first.

It had seemed like a great idea at the time. The only problem was, I forgot to mention to the school that we were doing it. Kids kept coming into the office with plastic bags filled with bottle caps, and Mrs. Insalaca thought it was an April Fool's Day joke. I don't think she believed me even after I explained it to her. Then she had to call all over the state to find a place that would recycle bottle caps.

I turned my attention back to Jamie. He kept saying, "But Dad . . . But Dad . . ." Finally he hung up the phone. "Dad says I can't sleep over on a school night."

"You have to," I whispered, pushing him out of the office. "I can't keep Amber awake all night by myself. Can't you sneak out?"

"I don't think so. This is my parents' favorite night for TV shows. They always make a huge bowl of popcorn and watch for two hours straight. They can see both the front and back doors from the living room."

"Then you'll have to climb out of the window."

Jamie stopped in his tracks. "Excuse me? Do I look like a crazy person?"

"Look," I said, "this is what friends are for. I'd help you save your pet if you asked me."

"Vera is a plant. I don't ask people to risk their lives to save her."

"Please, Jamie," I said in my most pitiful voice. That usually worked when everything else failed. "You wouldn't want me to lose my dog, would you? I might be scarred for life."

There was a long silence. "Okay . . . but if my parents catch us, you explain."

"Deal," I said. "I'll be outside your window at ten o'clock."

*   *   *

That night I left my jeans and T-shirt on under my pajamas when I went to bed. At 9:45, I snuck out of my room. Mom's door was closed. Just as I started down the stairs, Maxie came out of her room. "Where are you going?"

"To the bathroom."

"We have a bathroom up here."

"I know. I like the downstairs one better."

"You're lying." She pulled up the leg of my pajamas. "I thought so. You have your clothes on. You're sneaking out."

"Shhhh! Yes, but don't tell, okay?"

"Can I go, too?"

"No!"

Maxie took a step toward Mom's bedroom door. "Then I'm telling Mom what you're doing."

I didn't want her tagging along, but I was in enough trouble with Mom already. I pushed Maxie toward her room. "Okay, you can come with me, but you have to promise not to tell Mom afterward."

Maxie giggled and jumped up and down.

"This is serious stuff, Maxie."

"Okay. I promise."

"All right. Now get dressed quick."

It took Maxie forever to get ready. "Is it cold out?"

I stood by the door so I could watch Mom's room. "Shhh! I don't think so. What difference does it make?"

"Well, I've never been outside this late before. I don't know whether to wear a sweater or a sweatshirt."

"Either one is fine. Hurry up."

"But my red fuzzy sweater is warmer than my sweatshirt, so I need to know how cold it is before I —"

"Take them both," I said, grabbing her arm. "We're late."

By the time we put Amber on the leash and got to Jamie's, it was ten after ten. The first thing I noticed was something strange hanging from the tree outside Jamie's room.

It was Jamie.

Chapter Six

"Jamie! What are you doing?" I whispered.

"What does it look like I'm doing? Hanging! When I climbed out of my window, my belt got caught on a branch."

"Can't you reach back and get it unhooked?"

"Sure, and swing from the branch with one hand like a chimpanzee? I always fall in gym when they make us do the overhead ladder, remember?"

Maxie tugged on my sleeve. "If I stand on your shoulders, I can reach Jamie and get him loose."

"You're not climbing up on me, Maxie, so just forget it."

"You have any better ideas?" Jamie whispered. "Because if you keep standing there talking, my parents are going to hear you and come outside. That'll be the end of your big plan to save Amber."

"All right. Come on, Maxie." I crouched down and let Maxie climb on my back. Standing up wasn't easy, because she had a death grip on my head. "Get your hands off my eyes. I can't see!"

"Okay, okay!" Maxie said. "Hold still. I'm going to stand on your shoulders now."

She was pretty wobbly, so I had to keep sidestepping to keep her balanced. We must have looked like a circus act gone wrong. I staggered almost over to the sidewalk before we got lined up.

"Come back," Jamie said. "You can't leave me here. My parents are going to kill me."

"I'm trying." I started back toward the tree. "Maxie, don't lean forward."

I had to go faster to stay under her. "Stop leaning, Maxie. I mean it!" By the time we got to the tree, I was galloping. Amber thought it

was a game and lunged ahead, yanking on her leash.

That's when Maxie made a dive for Jamie's branch, and it broke.

"Yeeeeow!" Jamie yelled as the four of us collapsed in a heap in the bushes by the house. I lost my grip on Amber's leash and she took off. Suddenly Dr. Diggs appeared in the window. "What's going on out there?"

Amber barked. We all held our breath. "It was just a dog," Jamie's mother said.

We didn't breathe until Dr. Diggs had disappeared.

Jamie stood up and brushed the dirt off his jeans. "That was too close."

"Come on," I said. "Amber ran off. We have to catch her."

Jamie and I were halfway across the yard when I remembered Maxie. I went back and found her whimpering in the bushes.

"Come on, Maxie. Amber's getting away."

"I can't," Maxie said. "I think my leg is broken."

I slowly stood up and peeked in the window. Dr. Diggs was getting out of his chair. I crouched down next to Maxie. "Be quiet, Maxie. I'm going to carry you out of here, and then we'll check out your leg. I don't think it's really broken."

"Yes, it is," Maxie wailed.

"Maybe she's really hurt," Jamie said. "I'd better go in and get my mom and dad."

"Wait a minute," I said. "Maxie's always pretending she's hurt just to get Mom's attention. She's turning into a bigger con artist than me."

"I am not," Maxie wailed. "My leg is broken in three places. I can feel it."

"You're right," I said. "I can see a piece of your bone sticking out right where that big hairy spider is about to land on your leg."

Maxie took off like a shot, running all the way down to the streetlight.

"She heals fast," Jamie said.

"Yeah," I said. "Must be from all the vitamins Mom gives her."

Now with all the time we wasted on Maxie,

we had lost Amber. I started off down the street in the opposite direction, calling Amber's name softly.

Jamie ran to catch up to me. He looked over his shoulder. "We should go back for Maxie."

"Look," I said. "She shouldn't have come along in the first place. There's nothing wrong with her. I'm just worried about finding my dog."

I didn't have to worry long, because we found Amber at the next corner. I didn't have to worry about Maxie either, because she trotted right up behind us without even the slightest trace of a limp. Some broken leg.

"Okay," Jamie said. "Now that we're all back together, let's run and tire Amber out."

Maxie sat down on the grass. "I'm tired already. I want to go home."

"You wanted to come," I said. "Now you have to stay up." I took her hand.

We walked for blocks. Maxie was sure something scary was lurking behind every tree, waiting to ambush us. I tried not to think about it. None of us was used to being out this late. The whole neighborhood looked creepy.

"I can't keep going much longer," Jamie said finally.

I was getting tired, too, but one of us was still full of energy — Amber!

"Let's go to the beach," I said. "We can take turns running Amber so we won't all get worn out at once."

The beach was just at the end of our block, but I'd never seen it at night before. The tops of the waves sparkled in the moonlight. Maxie curled up in the sand and went right to sleep. I could tell she wasn't going to be much help, but at least she wouldn't be getting into trouble.

"I'll run Amber first," Jamie said. "You rest."

I stretched out and closed my eyes, listening to the waves. I must have fallen asleep, because it seemed as if Jamie was back two minutes later. "Your turn," he said as Amber licked my face.

I stumbled to my feet and took the leash.

Amber yanked me into motion. It was like a strange dream, being dragged down the beach in the dark. Everything looked purple and silver. I lurched along behind Amber, trying to stay on my feet. We ran the whole length of the beach four times. I was so tired, I could hardly stand up.

Jamie was snoring when I got back. I nudged him with my foot. "Your turn."

He rolled over. "Grugalumph."

"Wake up." I shook him, but he wouldn't budge.

"Okay, Amber," I said. "It's you and me." I couldn't run anymore, so I just walked her down the beach. I finally sat on a log to rest. Amber sat next to me, licking my face. "Maybe we don't have to keep moving," I said. "I just have to make sure you stay awake, that's all."

Amber thumped her tail as if she understood. I put my arm around her and nuzzled her ear. I loved the way she smelled. Mom said when I

was little, Amber used to let me curl up on the floor with her to take a nap. I used to rub the soft fur on the tips of her ears between my fingers to get to sleep. We have pictures of Amber with curly golden fur all over her except at the ends of her ears, where I had worn it off.

Tears stung my eyes. "Why do you have to be so much trouble? Can't you understand? All you have to do is behave yourself until I get home every day. Is that so hard?" I suddenly realized I was sounding just like Mom.

I wrapped the leash around my arm and stretched out on the sand. "I just need to rest, Amber. Then we'll run again." I tried not to close my eyes.

The next thing I knew, pink light streaked across the sky. I looked at my watch. It was six A.M.! Then I noticed something else. There was no leash wrapped around my arm. And there was no Amber! This time she was really gone.

Chapter Seven

There was no time to look for Amber, because Mom's alarm would be going off at 6:20. We had to be home and in our beds before she woke up. I dropped Jamie off at his house and helped him find the key hidden under a loose stone in the patio. He never could remember which one it was.

I had our house key with me. I unlocked the door slowly, and we slipped inside. Maxie wanted to go to sleep on the living room floor, so I had to carry her up the stairs. I put her to bed and had just jumped into my own bed and pulled the blanket up over my clothes when Mom knocked on my door and came in. "Time to get up, Sam."

"Okay, Mom. Don't worry about waking Maxie up. I'll do it for you."

"Thanks, Sam. Now I'll have a little extra time for myself." Mom messed up my hair and smiled. "Being considerate of other people is a sign of growing up, you know."

That made me feel rotten. The only reason I wanted to get Maxie up was because I put her to bed in her clothes. If Mom saw that, she'd start asking questions.

Mom did have a question, as soon as Maxie and I slid into our places at the kitchen table. "Sam, is Amber upstairs? She usually comes running when she hears me open the refrigerator."

Amber! I'd been so worried about Mom catching us, I'd forgotten all about her. "Amber?" I said, my mind racing. I was usually pretty good at making up fast excuses, but my brain felt numb from the lack of sleep. "Amber?"

Mom looked up from scrambling the eggs.

"Yes, Amber. You remember — blond hair, wet nose, long floppy ears . . ."

"Oh, well, Amber . . . uh . . . she . . ."

"Ran away," Maxie said.

Mom turned off the stove and sat down next to me. "How could she run away?"

"It must have been last night," I said, "when we were sleeping."

"On the beach," Maxie added.

Mom looked from Maxie to me. "Sleeping on the beach?"

There was no stopping Maxie after that. I just sat there, glassy-eyed, and listened to her blab everything to Mom. She even described the parts she had slept through!

Mom went back to the scrambled eggs. She was beating them so hard, little bits of egg were flying all over the stove. "I can't believe you did something so foolish. Who knows what might have happened to you kids, running all over in the middle of the night."

"I'm sorry, Mom," I said.

"Sorry doesn't cut it, Sam. It's too easy. You run around doing all kinds of outrageous things, then all you can say is 'I'm sorry'? You think that makes everything okay?" She banged the pan down on the table and slapped a clump of half-burned, half-runny eggs on my plate.

"No," I mumbled, wiping egg yolk off my shirt. "I know it's not okay."

"It's even more serious because you took Maxie along. Didn't you stop to think what might have happened to her?"

"I didn't want to take her, Mom. She's always butting in where she's not wanted."

Up until then, Maxie had been looking back and forth at our faces as if she were watching a Ping-Pong game, a big smile plastered across her face. She loved to hear Mom yell at me. "I do not butt in," she whined. "I have just as much right to do stuff as you do, Sam."

"Oh, yeah? Well I'm sick of having to take care of you all the time."

"Stop it, both of you!" Mom said. "You won't be having that problem from now on, Sam."

"What's that supposed to mean?"

"I've signed you both up for the Happy Days Day Care Center. You start this afternoon."

"Mom! Day care is for babies. Send Maxie if you want, but not me."

"You may think you're grown up, but you're too young to be left alone. Your actions have just proved that."

"But I only get in trouble because of Maxie and Amber. If I didn't have to worry about them, I'd be fine."

"Sam, you're going to Happy Days, and that's the end of it. I'll be working until five most days from now on. I've arranged to get out of work early this afternoon to take you there. After today, you'll know where it is. Your school bus goes right by it."

"But Mom!"

She handed me my lunch and a note. "Give

this to your teacher so she'll know I'm picking you up today. Now hurry up. I hear your bus coming."

I didn't think Jamie was on the bus at first because he had fallen asleep and was lying across a whole seat near the back.

"Wake up," I said, sliding into the seat with him.

Jamie tried to roll over. "Aw, Mom, please let me sleep a few more minutes."

Two fourth-grade girls sitting behind us started laughing at him. Jamie thrashed back in the other direction, almost kicking me in the face. This time I pulled him up into a sitting position.

"What . . . where am I?" he mumbled.

"You're on the school bus, making an idiot of yourself. What's the matter? You have amnesia or something?"

Jamie looked at me as if he didn't know who I was. Then his eyes narrowed. "You! I'm never speaking to you again."

"What happened? You didn't get caught, did you?"

"Caught? I almost got killed. As I was sneaking up the stairs, my father tried to hit me over the head with a baseball bat."

"Really? I guess I'm lucky. All my mother ever does is ground me."

"Dad wasn't trying to punish me, stupid. He thought I was a burglar. And if he had killed

71

his own son by mistake, he would have been scarred for life."

I snorted. "So would you!"

Jamie pushed past me to get out of the seat. "You think everything is a big joke, Sam. I'm through with you and your crazy schemes."

Jamie didn't speak to me all day in school. He wouldn't even look at me. Near the end of the day, Mrs. Insalaca's voice came over the intercom. "Ms. Lansing, would you please tell Sam he has a phone call in the office?"

I was usually glad for any excuse to get out of class, but a phone call in the office probably meant trouble. It was Mom. "Sam, the computer system at work went down. I can't get away even for a minute, so I can't pick you up at school."

My heart leapt. "Gee, that's a shame, Mom," I said, trying to sound disappointed. "I guess this means we don't get to go to the day care. I'll take Maxie home. Don't worry about a thing."

"I don't want you to go home, Sam. Everything has been arranged. Get on your regular school bus. Mrs. Insalaca is going to write a note to your driver telling him where you're supposed to get off. It's only three blocks past our house, on the same side of the street. There's a big yellow Happy Days sign out front."

"With a smiley face?" I mumbled.

"Yes! Do you know where it is?"

"No, that was just a lucky guess."

"Okay, Sam. I'm really sorry I can't take you in the first day, but I know you'll be fine. I'll pick you and Maxie up about five-twenty."

Jamie was still ignoring me when we got on the bus. I was glad, because he wouldn't see us staying on after our stop. I didn't want him to know I had to go to a baby day care. This was the most humiliating day of my life.

But maybe I wouldn't have to go after all. Maybe I'd get off at that stop to make sure Maxie got in all right. Then I'd keep walking and just run away. I leaned my head back on the seat and closed my eyes. I could see myself starting out on my new life. First thing I'd do was find Amber. Then the two of us would start looking for a home together. Maybe we wouldn't even need a home. We could sleep on the beach at night and eat weeds and berries. A person could survive on that. It was probably even healthy. Mom was always after me to eat green vegetables. Weeds were green, weren't they? Probably just loaded with vitamins.

The bus hit a pothole, and that brought me out of my daydream. I could see the stupid smiley-face sign half a block away from the stop. I held Maxie's hand as we got off the bus so people would think I was just taking my little sister to this stupid place. She jerked her hand away. "Knock it off, Sam. I'm not a baby."

"Okay, just go over to that lady by the front steps and tell her who you are."

"Why? Where are you going?"

"I'm not going anyplace," I lied. "If you think you're so big, I'm letting you go over there by yourself, that's all." I wanted to take off before the lady with the clipboard got to us.

Maxie's eyes filled with tears. "You can go with me if you want."

"You're big enough. I'll wait here." For a second I thought about having Maxie run away with me. No, that would never work. Maxie would barely eat good-tasting vegetables, like french fries. Fat chance of her eating weeds. I could see I was going to have to go in with her. She was really scared. Maxie didn't take too well to new situations.

The lady in charge introduced herself. Her name was Mrs. Monticello. "You must be Maxie and . . ." She looked at her clipboard.

"My brother's name is Sam," Maxie said.

Mrs. Monticello's face got red. "Oh, dear. According to the application your mother filled out, I was expecting you to be three years old, Sam. I assume you're not just big for your age."

I looked at the clipboard. "That's an eight. My mother has sloppy handwriting. Besides, I'm almost nine."

Mrs. Monticello smiled weakly. "Well, come on in, and we'll get Maxie settled."

I felt like a giant when we got inside. Little pairs of eyes stared from all over the room. I felt as if I'd been left back in school four years in a row. A teacher introduced Maxie to a bunch of kids playing in a toy kitchen. Maxie went right to work, pretending to wash dishes. Why couldn't she do that at home? I always got stuck with the job because Maxie was too little. Of course, having real water and breakable dishes might make a difference.

Mrs. Monticello looked around. "I'm afraid we aren't set up for anyone your age, Sam. Our oldest children are in kindergarten, like your sister. There's a latchkey program at the Y. It's for older kids who need a place to stay after school until their parents get home from work. I'll tell your mother about it when she comes to get you."

"The Y? Do they have sports and swimming?" I asked.

"I think they do," Mrs. Monticello said.

"You'll probably find quite a few of your class-mates there. For now, why don't you come with me to the senior room? You might enjoy our older members until your mother arrives."

As we went down the hall, Mrs. Monticello told me about Happy Days. Three different people stopped her with questions on the way, and she had to sign something for a delivery man. Each time she was interrupted in the middle of a sentence, she picked up right where she had left off.

When she opened the door at the end of the hall, I couldn't believe my eyes. The room was filled with people the age of my grandparents. A few of them were sitting next to playpens, playing with babies and toddlers. Some of them just stared into space. "How come you have grown-ups here?" I asked. "I thought day care was just for little kids."

"These people here aren't able to be home alone during the day," Mrs. Monticello said quietly. "Here they get a chance to be with children. The babies love the attention, so it works out well for everyone. Look, Sam. I think someone over there knows you."

I turned around. A man in the corner was waving at me.

"Mr. Watson!" I said, running over to hug him. "Am I ever glad to see you. What are you doing here?"

"My wife says I need to be here," he said. "I don't know why. I was happy at home."

"Me, too." I said. Seeing Mr. Watson made me remember Amber. I told him about how she ran away.

"Did I ever tell you about my dog, Midnight?" he asked. "He ran off one day. I looked all over for him."

"Did you ever find him?" I asked.

"Nope." He broke his oatmeal cookie and gave me half. "Midnight found me. I came home, and there he was, sitting on our front steps."

"I sure hope Amber can find me," I said.

But I was afraid she was lost forever.

Chapter Eight

Mom called the latchkey program, but they were filled up. "They've put you on the waiting list, Sam. Mrs. Monticello said you could stay at Happy Days for now, since it's an emergency."

"It's not an emergency, Mom. I could stay at home by myself."

"We've been all through this. You're too young to be left alone."

"But I'm too old to be at a day care with babies!"

"It's only for a little while," Mom said. "You'll just have to be patient."

I went out and sat on the back steps. Before, when Mom and I had had an argument about something, there were three things I could do.

First, I could tell Dad about it, and then he'd go talk Mom over to my side. If that didn't work, I'd tell Jamie, and sometimes he could come up with a way to get around Mom. If that didn't work, I'd go toss a Frisbee around with Amber. She didn't have any answers, but it always made me feel better.

I picked up the bright orange Frisbee and ran my fingers over Amber's teeth marks. Now Dad and Amber were gone, and Jamie might never speak to me again. To make matters worse, I was still grounded, so I couldn't go looking for Amber on my own. Mom took me out a couple of times in the car to look for her, but I wanted to search out hiding places. You have to be walking to do that. I knew we'd never find Amber. My life was a total mess.

My life wasn't the only thing that was a mess. The big tree in the backyard had shed most of its leaves. Dad and I used to rake the leaves together every fall, then put them in bags out at the curb. Mom didn't have time to do any stuff in the yard now that she had her job.

There were branches all over from a windstorm two weeks ago. I looked in the garage and found the rakes and even a box of bags. Before I realized I was working, I had filled three bags with leaves. As I was dragging the last fallen branch to a pile at the curb, Mom came out.

"Sam, you're an angel. I can't believe you did all this without being asked." She hugged me. "This is exactly what I meant when I said we needed to work together as a family. You're really growing up."

Mom's words made me feel good for a while, but it didn't last. The only thing I had to look forward to was getting into the after-school program at the Y. At least that would be better than sitting around at Happy Days waiting for my mother to pick us up. There wasn't even anything to look forward to when I got home, because Jamie still wasn't speaking to me.

*   *   *

The next day at Happy Days, the people in the senior room were mostly staring into space or sleeping. Even Mr. Watson didn't feel like talking. I finally got bored and went back in with the little kids. There was a new boy about Maxie's age who was scared. A teacher was trying to calm him down, but he wouldn't stop crying. I started making funny faces at him from across the room. He pretended not to notice at first, but pretty soon he couldn't help smiling.

The teacher looked up and figured out what was going on. She brought him over to me. "Sam, this is Jason. This is his first day here. I bet he'd love to have you read a book to him."

"Hi, Jason. Sure. Let's find a good book." At least that might help the time pass faster. Jason wiped his nose on his sleeve and nodded. I took him over to the bookshelf, and he picked out a book about a boy who loves trucks. I sat on the floor and started reading. Pretty soon some other little kids sat down to listen. When I finished, a little girl ran over to the bookcase and came back with her favorite book. More

kids gathered around — even Maxie. Before I knew it, I had a pile of six books next to me, and it was time for the parents to start picking up the kids. "What's this? A new teacher?" one of the fathers asked.

"That's Sam," Maxie said. "He's my big brother." She sounded proud when she said it. That was a first!

*   *   *

Mom finally agreed to let Maxie and me look for Amber over the weekend. I made a map of all the streets in our neighborhood. Maxie carried it on a clipboard and checked off each house as we searched. I showed a picture of Amber to everyone we met. Nobody had seen her.

That Monday when we got on the bus after school, Jamie started speaking to me again. "Come sit back here, Sam. I saved you a seat." There was one good thing about Jamie. As soon as he got over being mad, it was like nothing had ever happened. "I'd ask you to come over this afternoon, but I'm going to my cousin's. Want to come over tomorrow after school?"

"I can't," I said. At first I was going to make up some kind of excuse so Jamie wouldn't know about the day care center. Then I realized his cousin's house was a couple of stops past Happy Days, so he'd see where we got off. It was so good to be talking to Jamie again, I decided to tell him the whole story.

"The day care center?" he asked. "Isn't that just for little kids?"

"Yeah. It was a big mix-up. They thought I was younger. I won't be there for long, though. As soon as there's an opening, I get to go to the Y. They probably have all kinds of sports."

"I don't see why you just can't come over to my house," Jamie said. "My dad's always there. He wouldn't mind if you were there."

"I know, but Mom says you and I get in too much trouble."

Jamie looked out of the window. "Parents can be so unfair. We just — hey, Sam! Look who's on your front steps!"

It was Amber. When she saw the school bus, she trotted out to meet it, her tail wagging like a flag. "Jamie, make sure Maxie gets off at the day care — the place with the big smiley face. There's a lady who waits for the kids to get off the bus. Maxie, tell Mrs. Monticello I'll be a little late. I have to get Amber before she runs away again." I jumped off the bus with the other kids from our stop. The driver was a substitute and never noticed.

"Amber! Where have you been?" She had burrs stuck all over her coat and she smelled like a swamp, but I didn't care. I hugged her until I thought my arms would fall off. And she licked my face and ears so hard she made my hair damp around the edges.

"You're hungry, aren't you? I can't get in the house to feed you, because Mom took away my key."

I gave her a drink from the garden hose.

Then I knocked on the Watsons' door to see if I could use their phone to call Mom, but nobody was home. I grabbed what was left of Amber's leash and started toward Happy Days. When we got to the corner, I stopped at Levinson's Market. Mr. Levinson let me have some Doggy Burgers when I told him what had happened.

"I'll pay you as soon as Mom comes home, Mr. Levinson."

"That's okay, Sam. It can be a welcome-home present from me to Amber." Amber wolfed down the burgers almost whole, and Mr. Levinson gave her some more water.

When we got to Happy Days, Mrs. Monticello met me at the door. "Sam! I was about to send someone off to look for you."

"Didn't Maxie tell you I was going to be late?"

"Yes, but you're my responsibility. I couldn't just let you wander around."

"I wasn't wandering around, and Amber is

my responsibility and she ran away a few days ago but she came back and was sitting on our front steps just the way Mr. Watson's Midnight did and I couldn't just leave her because she'd only run away again and I'm trying to find a new home for her and I —"

Mrs. Monticello put her hands on my shoulders. "Whoa, Sam, stop to take a breath."

"Can I stay outside with Amber until Mom comes?" I asked. "We won't go anywhere. I promise."

Mrs. Monticello reached down to pet Amber. "She seems like a nice dog. Why are you giving her away?"

I told her about the barking.

"Oh, I see," she said. "Well, we can't leave the two of you out here. Bring her in. Just make sure she doesn't get into any trouble."

Mr. Watson's eyes lit up as Amber came into the senior room. "Sam, your dog is back."

"She was on the front steps, Mr. Watson. Just like you said. Just like Midnight."

Mr. Watson scratched Amber behind the ears. "She's got some burrs here. We'd better work on her."

He took a comb out of his pocket and set to work, gently pulling out the tangles. A white-haired lady had been sitting next to us, staring into space. She reached out to touch Amber. "Dog," she said. "Pretty dog." Amber licked the lady's hand.

"Amber, cut it out," I said. "You're going to get us into trouble." I reached for her leash, but Mr. Watson stopped me.

"Leave her be, Sam. She just wants to make friends."

A lady in a wheelchair across the room called to Amber, and Amber trotted over, her tail wagging. Then she stopped to say hello to everybody around the room.

Finally she came back to the white-haired lady and settled down at her feet. "Dog," the lady said, smiling at Amber. "Pretty, pretty dog."

"That's Emma," Mr. Watson said. "Funny, I've never heard her say anything before."

"I just had the greatest idea, Mr. Watson. Amber makes people happy. She could come here every day. This could be her job!"

I ran into the little kids' room and told Mrs. Monticello about my idea. Maxie came over when she saw me.

"I'm sorry, Sam." Mrs. Monticello said. "I know Amber's a great dog, but I can't have her here all the time. She might hurt one of the children by accident."

"But she's great with children, Mrs. Monticello. She's been with me and Maxie since we were born."

"That's right," Maxie said, "and we're both children."

"Sam, I know it would be nice for you to have your dog here." Mrs. Monticello put her arm around my shoulder. "I'm sure it's hard not having anyone your age. The latchkey program is expanding. They should be able to take you soon."

"But I'm not doing this for me, Mrs. Monticello. It's for Amber. If she had a place to go while Mom was at work, we wouldn't have to get rid of her." I told her about all the things Jamie and I had tried to keep Amber quiet at home.

Mrs. Monticello shook her head. "I'd like help, Sam, but we don't take care of animals here. What if Amber should bite someone?"

"She wouldn't. Amber's never bitten anybody in her life."

Mrs. Monticello smiled and patted me on the head. "There's a first time for everything, Sam."

Maxie looked up at Mrs. Monticello and frowned. It was a good thing I was going to the Y pretty soon, because right then I wanted to bite Mrs. Monticello myself!

Chapter Nine

Mom was as glad to see Amber as I was. Amber was so excited to have the family together, she jumped all over the backseat of the car going home. When we got there, I fed her a big meal and took her out to the backyard. I was playing Frisbee with her when I heard the front doorbell. Mom yelled from the kitchen. "Answer that, will you, Sam? My hands are full of raw meat loaf."

I ran through the house, and when I opened the door, Meredith Rumsey was standing there. "Hi, Samuel. I came to visit Amber."

With all the excitement about Amber coming home, I'd forgotten about Meredith. I knew now I could never give Amber up, no matter what. Meredith started to barge right in, but I blocked her way. "You can't visit Amber. She's . . . um . . . lost."

"Oh, yeah? So who's barking in the backyard, your sister?"

"The deal's off, Meredith. Amber's my dog."

Meredith's eyes narrowed. "She's going to be *my* dog very soon. If I can't see her now, you can't visit her when she's mine."

"Oh, Meredith." Mom came into the room, wiping her hands on a dish towel. I could tell from the expression on her face that she'd forgotten about Meredith, too. "Did you come to see Amber?"

"Yes, ma'am. I want her to be used to me when I take her home on Saturday."

"Mom, she can't have Amber. Not after everything that's happened. Not after losing her and finding her again."

"We had an agreement," Mom said. "I guess it wouldn't be fair to back out of it now."

"My father would be mad if you did," Meredith said. "He's worked really hard fencing in our yard for Amber."

"He should use the fence to keep *you* penned up," I said, "instead of letting you run all over the neighborhood annoying people."

I smelled raw meat loaf as Mom put her hand on my shoulder. "I'm sure your father has put a lot of effort into the fence project, Meredith. And I apologize for the way Sam is acting. He's just upset about giving up Amber."

"I'm *not* giving her up," I said. "Not in a million years."

Mom's grip tightened. "Meredith, why don't you go play with Amber for a while? She's out back."

Meredith gave me an "I told you so" look as she pushed past me and went outside. I glared back.

"There's no way I'm letting her have my dog, Mom. When Amber ran away this week, it was worse than when Arnie Sanderson moved away." Arnie had been my best friend in kindergarten and first grade. I didn't feel like smiling for weeks after he left.

Mom put her arms around me. "Sam, I

know how you feel, but I don't see any other way. At least if Meredith has Amber, you'll get to see her."

"You don't understand. Meredith Rumsey is the rottenest person in the whole world. Besides, you said we're all going to have to work together around here. Why can't we all work together to save Amber? Every idea you've come up with is to get rid of her."

Mom pulled back the curtain and watched Amber bounding around the backyard with Meredith. "She *has* been a part of the family for a long time."

"That's right!" Mom was weakening. Now if I could only convince her. I bolted for the bookcase and pulled out the old family album. I flipped through the pages until I came to the picture of Amber with her worn-out ears. "Look, Mom. Remember how I used to take naps with Amber?"

Mom laughed. "She was your security blanket. It's a good thing you outgrew naps, or the poor dog would have been bald."

I led her over to the couch and put the big scrapbook across both of our laps. There were as many pictures of Amber as there were of me and Maxie. "Amber's a part of our lives, Mom. You can't give away a member of the family just because she's caused problems. Maxie's been a pain all her life, and we still have *her*."

"But Mr. Rumsey has gone to all that trouble building the fence. . . ."

"Mom, there are seventeen zillion dogs at the pound who need homes. Nobody even wants them. The Rumseys would be doing a

good deed if they took one."

Mom sighed. "You're right, Sam. But that doesn't solve the problem of Amber's barking. The Rumseys are Amber's only hope for a new home. Nobody else answered the ad."

"We still have until Saturday. Just try to come up with a plan, Mom. I have one idea that might work. I'm going to Jamie's."

If anybody could help me, it was Dr. Diggs. He was out in the driveway washing the car when I got there. "Jamie's not here right now, Sam," he said.

"That's okay, Dr. Diggs. You're the one I wanted to see. I need your help with a problem."

Dr. Diggs ducked around the other side of the car when he saw Amber. "I . . . uh . . . thought you weren't going to bring your dog over here anymore, Sam."

"I'm sorry, Dr. Diggs. I might have Amber only a few more days, so I want to spend as much time with her as I can."

Dr. Diggs peeked over the roof of the car.

Amber was sitting quietly, wagging her tail. "Well, your dog does seem much calmer today."

"She's usually like this," I said. "She was just excited when you saw her the other day. You don't need to be afraid of her."

Dr. Diggs took a few steps toward Amber. "What problem did you want to ask me about?"

I told him about the day care center. "Amber made friends with a lady named Emma. Mr. Watson said he'd never heard her talk before, but she did when Amber went up to her."

Dr. Diggs nodded. "That wouldn't surprise me. I've read about a number of cases like that in medical journals. Some patients will respond to an animal when nobody else can reach them."

"Really? Could you give me one of those journals so I could show it to Mrs. Monticello?"

"Come on into the office, and I'll see what I can find for you, Sam." I had Amber wait on

101

the front steps while we went inside. Dr. Diggs flipped through a pile of magazines in his bookcase. "Ah, here it is. This ought to help your cause."

I thanked Dr. Diggs and ran all the way home with the magazine. I tried to read the article that night. It had a lot of big words that I didn't understand, but it told about how animals had helped people in nursing homes and some patients in mental hospitals.

It was easy to imagine Amber helping the older people at the day care center. After all, Amber loved people so much, she couldn't stand to be without them. Mrs. Monticello couldn't argue with an official article like this. My problems were almost over. Meredith Rumsey would have to find herself another dog.

Chapter Ten

I showed the magazine to Mrs. Monticello the minute Maxie and I arrived at Happy Days the next afternoon.

"This article tells about how dogs help people in nursing homes. I know Amber could do the same thing here."

"That sounds interesting, Sam. But I can't read it right now. I have to go spread peanut butter on graham crackers for the afternoon snack. I'll take the article home to read tonight."

Maxie tugged on Mrs. Monticello's sleeve. "We can't wait that long. Sam makes snacks for me all the time. You can read while he spreads peanut butter."

Mrs. Monticello smiled and led us into the

kitchen. "So you're ganging up on me. All right, you win." She sat on a stool by the counter and started reading.

"Thanks," I whispered to Maxie.

"You're not the only one who grew up with Amber," she whispered back.

I tried to be as neat as I could with the pea-

nut butter while I watched Mrs. Monticello out of the corner of my eye. I didn't even lick my fingers. We finished at the same time.

"This article is very interesting, Sam, but we couldn't have Amber here without supervision. She can be here after school, as long as you're here to watch her. You'll have to figure out a way to get her here."

"That's great, Mrs. Monticello. I'll get her here." That was a start. Then, when I started at the Y, she could go with me. But Amber would still be alone every day until two o'clock.

When Mom picked us up that day, she had a package next to her on the seat. What's that?" I asked, sliding in next to her.

"It's a surprise," she said. "It may help with our Amber problem."

I tried to get her to explain, but she wouldn't. When we got home, Mom hooked up some cables between the phone, her computer, and the little gray plastic box.

"Amber's smart, Mom, but I know she can't

use a computer. Her paws are too big to hit the little keys."

Mom laughed. "This is a modem, Sam. Watch this." She brought something up on her computer screen and typed a number. There was one high-pitched sound followed by another. The word *Connected* came up on the screen.

"I don't get it," I said.

"My computer has called the computer at work. I'm going to have my boss send a file to me. She stayed late so we could test the system."

Mom typed, "Hi, Alice. Try sending me the September sales graph." I watched as the screen filled with a graph.

"That's great, Mom, but what does it have to do with Amber?"

"Now I can work on this at home and send it back by modem," Mom said. "I can send information from my computer to the one at the office through the phone."

"You mean you'll be working at home from now on?" Maxie asked.

"Not every day. There are meetings I have to attend, and other things that have to be done in the office. We're rearranging the schedule so I can work at home on Tuesdays and Thursdays."

"That's great, Mom." I told her about the deal I made with Mrs. Monticello. "Is it okay with you if I get off the bus and walk Amber to the day care? I did it the day she was lost, and it wasn't bad. It's only a couple of blocks past Jamie's house and I go over there all the time."

Mom smiled. "I guess that would be all right. Any boy who tries as hard as you have to keep his dog should be allowed to do it. We just need to figure out what to do with Amber the other three days of the week until you get home from school. I wish they had baby-sitters for dogs."

After dinner, I went over to Jamie's to return the magazine.

Jamie answered the door. "What's happening with Amber? Will they let her stay at the day care?"

"Only after school while I'm there. Can you come out? Amber's with me."

Dr. Diggs came to the door. "You can bring your dog in, Sam. She seemed very well behaved yesterday. I really should get used to dogs." He walked over to Amber, reached out his hand, then pulled it back.

"Go ahead, pet her," I said. "She has real silky ears."

Dr. Diggs sat down in an overstuffed chair. Amber trotted over to him. "I've never let myself get this close to a dog before," he said, petting Amber with one finger. "I can see how you might grow attached to one. She is really quite friendly."

Amber's tail thumped happily against the coffee table.

I cleared my throat. "I read that article you gave me."

Dr. Diggs looked up, surprised. "Really?"

"Well," I said, "most of it. Especially the part about how dogs help people in mental hospitals. Isn't that the kind of patients you have coming in here, Dr. Diggs?"

"My patients have problems, Sam. They come here to talk them over with me."

This was a real long shot, but it was my last hope. I took a deep breath and plunged in. "Don't you think your patients would like to pet a dog while they talked about their problems?" I asked. "I know it always helps me."

Dr. Diggs smiled at Amber. "I can see how it might be comforting." He was scratching her behind the ears now.

"That's a great idea, Dad," Jamie said. "You could have Amber here until we get home from school."

Dr. Diggs held up his hands. "Now don't get carried away. I said I should get used to dogs. I didn't say I wanted one around here all the time."

"It wouldn't be every day, Dr. Diggs. My mom is staying home two days a week, so we just need a place for Mondays, Wednesdays, and Fridays."

Dr. Diggs shook his head. "Well, I really don't think I could. . . ."

Jamie put his arm around my shoulders. "Dad, if Sam doesn't get someone to watch Amber, he's going to have to give her away.

Losing your dog like that could scar a kid for life, couldn't it?"

"Why didn't you tell me you'd have to give up your dog, Sam? Maybe Amber and I could get along a few days a week."

"Really?" I said. "You wouldn't mind?"

Dr. Diggs smiled at Jamie. "Yes, I mind, but I don't want to be responsible for scarring my son's best friend for life. Bring Amber over in the morning. We'll give it a try."

That night, Mom made me call Mr. Rumsey and explain about not wanting to give up my dog. It was a hard call to make, but it was worth it. Amber was still mine!

Chapter Eleven

I got off the bus at Jamie's the next day to pick Amber up. Dr. Diggs said his patients didn't mind having a dog around. Most of them even liked it.

The people at Happy Days liked having Amber around, too. When I took her into the senior room, Mr. Watson was just sitting there, staring again. But as soon as he saw Amber, his face broke into a big smile. Amber seemed to know she had a job to do at Happy Days. She didn't jump up on anybody as she went around the room saying hello to people.

Later that afternoon, Mrs. Monticello came into the senior room with Jason and a couple of his friends. "The children wanted to come in and have you read to them, Sam. Could you manage to keep an eye on Amber and read at the same time?"

"Sure. Amber's no problem. Besides, Mr. Watson is watching her now." Mr. Watson had taken Amber over to a man in a wheelchair on the far side of the room. They were telling each other stories about the pets they had as kids. "People sure do respond to your dog, Sam," Mrs. Monticello said. "And you've made quite a hit with some of our children. Jason has been carrying the truck book around all day. Several staff members have offered to read it to him, but he said he was waiting for you."

Every day that week, I read to the little kids while Amber made the rounds of the seniors. She always saved Emma for last, nuzzling her arm until Emma petted her.

Sometimes we played games and the seniors helped the kids. Everybody's favorite was animal bingo. The kids paired up with the seniors and helped each other watch the cards as I called off the animals. The time went by so fast

some days, I thought Mom was getting out of work early.

On Tuesdays and Thursdays I was home like the old days. It was good to go over to Jamie's after school again. One day while I was at Jamie's, I got a call from Mom. "A spot has opened up for you at the latchkey program, Sam. You can start tomorrow. The program sounds wonderful. They have all kinds of sports and craft activities — even swimming and movies."

"That's great," I said.

"What's great?" Jamie asked.

"I start at the Y tomorrow. I can take Amber with me, can't I, Mom?"

"That's a problem," Mom said. "They don't allow pets. I couldn't talk them into changing their minds."

"Then I can't go. I'll have to stay at Happy Days."

Jamie punched me in the arm. "What, are you crazy? I'll watch Amber after school for you. I always wanted a dog anyway. You don't want to stay at the baby day care, do you?"

"You sure your dad won't mind?"

"Mind? He's crazy about Amber. She got him over his dog phobia."

"Mom, Jamie says he'll watch Amber after school. Can I go one last time to Happy Days to say good-bye to everybody?"

"I'm sure it won't be a problem. I'll call both places to make arrangements."

The next day, Mrs. Monticello had made a cake that said, "Good-bye, Sam and Amber"

on the top in big red letters. She had drawn a picture of Amber and me, too, but it was hard to tell what it was. Mrs. Monticello wasn't a great artist, especially in frosting.

After we had our cake, I started to take Amber into the senior room. That's when I heard someone crying. It was Jason.

"What's the matter, Jason?" I asked.

He turned his back to me. Mrs. Monticello came over. "Jason's been upset ever since he heard you wouldn't be coming anymore, Sam. Don't worry, though. He'll get over it. Why don't you take Amber in to say good-bye to the seniors?"

"But maybe if I read the truck book to him —"

Jason started crying even harder.

Mrs. Monticello led me toward the door. "It will be easier if he doesn't see you, Sam."

Mr. Watson had saved his piece of cake for Amber. She took it gently from his hand, licking the crumbs and frosting from his fingers.

"Won't be the same around here without you, Sam," Mr. Watson said. "We're going to miss our visits with Amber, too."

"You'll still see us at home," I said, but I knew it wasn't the same. And none of the other people would get to see Amber at all after today.

"Sam will be going to the Y from now on," Mrs. Monticello said. "He'll be with kids his own age, and they have all kinds of great activities, right, Sam?"

"Yeah, I guess so." I watched Amber making her rounds. Each person's face brightened up as Amber stopped to be petted. She came back to Emma last, putting her head in the old woman's lap.

"I had a dog named Midnight," Mr. Watson said to Emma. It was probably the hundredth time he'd told her. "Midnight was black with pointy ears."

Emma slowly ran her hand over Amber's velvety head. "My dog was Kaiser," she said, so quietly we could barely hear her. "White with brown spots. Soft, like this dog."

I knew right then I wasn't going to leave Happy Days.

Amber and I have been "volunteers" for almost the whole school year now. Amber has Emma talking so much, they can't shut her up. Every time Mr. Watson tries to tell stories about Midnight, Emma starts right in about her dog, Kaiser.

Jason can read the truck book out loud to the other kids. He cheats, though. I think he has it memorized.

Even Maxie doesn't seem quite so bratty anymore. It's like I keep telling Mom: Being responsible for a pet really matures a person. Hmm. Maybe we should get Maxie a dog of her own. . . .